D0040919

ALMOST MIDNIGHT

Also by Rainbow Rowell

Carry On

Fangirl

Attachments

Eleanor & Park

Landline

ALMOST MIDNIGHT

two festive short stories by

RAINBOW ROWELL

illustrated by SIMINI BLOCKER

MACMILLAN

'Midnights' first published 2014 in *My True Love Gave to Me* in the US by St. Martin's Press and in the UK by Macmillan Children's Books; 'Kindred Spirits' first published 2016 for World Book Day by Macmillan Children's Books

This edition published 2017 by Macmillan Children's Books
an imprint of Pan Macmillan
20 New Wharf Road, London N1 9RR
Associated companies throughout the world
www.panmacmillan.com

ISBN 978-1-5098-6994-7 (HB)
ISBN 978-1-5098-8600-5 (TPB)

1 3 5 7 9 8 6 4 2

A CIP catalogue record for this book is available fromthe British Library.

Printed and bound by CPI Group (UK) Ltd, Croydon CR0 4YY

Contents

MIDNIGHTS

December 2016, almost [illegible]

[illegible] was cold out on the patio [illegible]
[illegible] frigid. Dark.

[illegible] dark because Mags [illegible]
midnight and dark because [illegible]
[illegible]

This was the last place [illegible]
[illegible] anyone until [illegible]
[illegible] the excitement.

[illegible] Mags [illegible]
the birthday age.

[illegible] leaned back against [illegible]
started eating the Chex mix [illegible]
[illegible] Alicia's mom made [illegible]
[illegible] hear the music [illegible]
[illegible] couldn't [illegible] and that [illegible]
[illegible] that the countdown [illegible]
[illegible] she heard someone [illegible]
[illegible] more people joined [illegible]

[illegible] was going to miss the [illegible]
[illegible]

31 December 2014, *almost midnight*

It was cold out on the patio, under the deck. Frigid. Dark.

Dark because Mags was outside at midnight, and dark because she was in the shadows.

This was the last place anyone would look for her—anyone, and especially Noel. She'd miss all the excitement.

Thank God. Mags should have thought of this years ago.

She leaned back against Alicia's house and started eating the Chex mix she'd brought out with her. (Alicia's mom made the best Chex mix.) Mags could hear the music playing inside, and then she couldn't—and that was a good sign. It meant that the countdown was starting.

'Ten!' she heard someone shout.

'Nine!' more people joined in.

'Eight!'

Mags was going to miss the whole thing.

Perfect.

31 December 2011, *almost midnight*

'Are there nuts in that?' the boy asked.

Mags paused, holding a cracker piled with pesto and cream cheese in front of her mouth. 'I think there are pine nuts . . .' she said, crossing her eyes to look at it.

'Are pine nuts tree nuts?'

'I have no idea,' Mags said. 'I don't think pine nuts grow on pine trees, do they?'

The boy shrugged. He had shaggy brown hair and wide-open blue eyes. He was wearing a Pokémon T-shirt.

'I'm not much of a tree-nut expert,' Mags said.

'Me neither,' he said. 'You'd think I would be—if I accidentally eat one, it could kill me. If there were something out there that could kill you, wouldn't you try to be an expert on it?'

'I don't know. . . .' Mags shoved the cracker in her mouth and started chewing. 'I don't know very much about cancer. Or car accidents.'

'Yeah . . .' the boy said, looking sadly at the buffet table. He was skinny. And pale. 'But tree nuts specifically have it out for me, for me *personally*. They're more like assassins than, like, possible dangers.'

'Damn,' Mags said, 'what'd you ever do to tree nuts?'

The boy laughed. 'Ate them, I guess.'

The music, which had been really loud, stopped. 'It's almost midnight!' somebody shouted.

They both looked around. Mags's friend Alicia, from homeroom, was standing on the couch. It was Alicia's party—the first New Year's Eve party that Mags, at fifteen, had ever been invited to.

'Nine!' Alicia yelled.

'Eight!' There were a few dozen people in the basement, and they were all shouting now.

'Seven!'

'I'm Noel,' the boy said, holding out his hand.

Mags brushed all the pesto and traces of nuts off her hand and shook his. 'Mags.'

'Four!'

'Three!'

'It's nice to meet you, Mags.'

'You, too, Noel. Congratulations on evading the tree nuts for another year.'

'They almost had me with that pesto dip.'

'Yeah.' She nodded. 'It was a close call.'

31 December 2012, *almost midnight*

Noel fell against the wall and slid down next to Mags, then bumped his shoulder against hers. He blew a paper party horn in her direction. 'Hey.'

'Hey.' She smiled at him. He was wearing a plaid jacket, and his white shirt was open at the collar. Noel was pale and flushed easily. Right now he was pink from the top of his forehead to the second button of his shirt. 'You're a dancing machine,' she said.

'I like to dance, Mags.'

'I know you do.'

'And I only get so many opportunities.'

She raised an eyebrow.

'I like to dance *in public,*' Noel said. 'With other people. It's a communal experience.'

'I kept your tie safe,' she said, and held out a red silk necktie. He'd been dancing on the coffee table when he threw it at her.

'Thank you,' he said, taking it and slinging it around his neck. 'That was a good catch—but I was actually trying to lure you out onto the dance floor.'

'That was a coffee table, Noel.'

'There was room for two, Margaret.'

Mags wrinkled her nose, considering. 'I don't think there was.'

'There's always room for you with me, on every coffee table,' he said. 'Because you are my best friend.'

'Pony is your best friend.'

Noel ran his fingers through his hair. It was sweaty and curly and fell past his ears. 'Pony is also my best friend. And also Frankie. And Connor.'

'And your mom,' Mags said.

Noel turned his grin on her. 'But especially you. It's our anniversary. I can't believe you wouldn't dance with me on our anniversary.'

'I don't know what you're talking about,' she

said. (She knew exactly what he was talking about.)

'It happened right there.' Noel pointed at the buffet table where Alicia's mom always laid out snacks. 'I was having an allergic reaction, and you saved my life. You stuck an epinephrine pen into my heart.'

'I ate some pesto,' Mags said.

'Heroically,' Noel agreed.

She sat up suddenly. 'You didn't eat any of the chicken salad tonight, did you? There were almonds.'

'Still saving my life,' he said.

'*Did* you?'

'No. But I had some fruit cocktail. I think there were strawberries in it—my mouth is all tingly.'

Mags squinted at him. 'Are you okay?'

Noel looked okay. He looked flushed. And sweaty. He looked like his teeth were too wide for his mouth, and his mouth was too wide for his face.

'I'm fine,' he said. 'I'll tell you if my tongue gets puffy.'

'Keep your lewd allergic reactions to yourself,' she said.

Noel wiggled his eyebrows. 'You should see what happens when I eat shellfish.'

Mags rolled her eyes and tried not to laugh. After a second, she looked over at him again. 'Wait, what happens when you eat shellfish?'

He waved his hand in front of his chest, halfheartedly. 'I get a rash.'

She frowned. '*How* are you still alive?'

'Through the efforts of everyday heroes like yourself.'

'Don't eat the pink salad, either,' she said. 'It's shrimp.'

Noel flicked his red tie around her neck and smiled at her. Which was different than a grin. 'Thanks.'

'Thank *you,*' she said, pulling the ends of the tie even and looking down at them. 'It matches my sweater.' Mags was wearing a giant sweater dress, some sort of Scandinavian design with a million colors.

'Everything matches your sweater,' he said. 'You look like a Christmas-themed Easter egg.'

'I feel like a really colorful Muppet,' she said.

'One of the fuzzy ones.'

'I like it,' Noel said. 'It's a feast for the senses.'

She couldn't tell if he was making fun of her, so she changed the subject. 'Where did Pony go?'

'Over there.' Noel pointed across the room. 'He wanted to get in position to be standing casually near Simini when midnight strikes.'

'So he can kiss her?'

'Indeed,' Noel said. 'On the mouth, if all goes to plan.'

'That's so gross,' Mags said, fiddling with the ends of Noel's tie.

'Kissing?'

'No . . . kissing is fine.' She felt herself blushing. Fortunately she wasn't as pale as Noel; it wouldn't be painted all over her face and throat. 'What's gross is using New Year's Eve as an excuse to kiss someone who might want not want to kiss you. Using it as a trick.'

'Maybe Simini *does* want to kiss Pony.'

'Or maybe it'll be really awkward,' Mags said. 'And she'll do it anyway because she feels like she has to.'

'He's not going to maul her,' Noel said. 'He'll do the eye contact thing.'

'What eye contact thing?'

Noel swung his head around and made eye contact with Mags. He raised his eyebrows hopefully; his eyes went all soft and possible. It was definitely a face that said, *Hey. Is it okay if I kiss you?*

'Oh,' Mags said. 'That's really good.'

Noel snapped out of it—and made a face that said, *Well, duh.* 'Of course it's good. I've kissed girls before.'

'*Have* you?' Mags asked. She knew that Noel talked to girls. But she'd never heard of him having a girlfriend. And she *would* have heard of it—she was one of Noel's four to five best friends.

'Pfft,' he said. 'Three girls. Eight different occasions. I think I know how to make eye contact.'

That was significantly more kissing than Mags had managed in her sixteen years.

She glanced over at Pony again. He was standing near the television, studying his phone. Simini was a few feet away, talking to her friends.

'Still,' Mags said, 'it feels like cheating.'

'How is it cheating?' Noel asked, following her eyes. 'Neither of them is in a relationship.'

'Not that kind of cheating,' Mags said. 'More

like . . . skipping ahead. If you like someone, you should have to make an effort. You should have to get to know the person—you should have to *work* for that first kiss.'

'Pony and Simini already know each other.'

'Right,' she agreed, 'and they've never gone out. Has Simini ever even *indicated* that she's interested?'

'Sometimes people need help,' Noel said. 'I mean—look at Pony.'

Mags did. He was wearing black jeans and a black T-shirt. He had a half-grown-out mohawk now, but he'd had a ponytail back in middle school, so everyone still called him that. Pony was usually loud and funny, and sometimes loud and obnoxious. He was always drawing on his arm with ink pens.

'That guy has no idea how to tell a girl he likes her,' Noel said. 'None at all. . . . Now, look at Simini.'

Mags did. Simini was small and soft, and so shy that coming out of her shell wasn't even on the menu. If you wanted to talk to Simini, you had to climb inside her shell with her.

'Not everyone has our social graces,' Noel said, sighing, and leaning into Mags's space to gesture toward Pony and Simini. 'Not everyone knows how to reach out for the things they want. Maybe midnight is exactly what these two need to get rolling—would you begrudge them that?'

Mags turned to Noel. His face was just over her shoulder. He smelled warm. And like some sort of Walgreens body spray. 'You're being melodramatic,' she said.

'Life-or-death situations bring it out in me.'

'Like coffee table dancing?'

'No, the strawberries,' he said, sticking out his tongue and trying to talk around it. 'Duth it look puffy?'

Mags was trying to get a good look at Noel's tongue when the music dropped out.

'It's almost midnight!' Alicia shouted, standing near the television. The countdown was starting in Times Square. Mags saw Pony look up from his phone and inch toward Simini.

'Nine!' the room shouted.

'Eight!'

'Your tongue looks fine,' Mags said, turning back to Noel.

He pulled his tongue back in his mouth and smiled.

Mags raised her eyebrows. She hardly realized she was doing it. 'Happy anniversary, Noel.'

Noel's eyes went soft. At least, she thought they did. 'Happy anniversary, Mags.'

'Four!'

And then Natalie ran over, slid down the wall next to Noel, and grabbed his shoulder.

Natalie was friends with both of them, but she wasn't a *best* friend. She had caramel-brown hair, and she always wore flannel shirts that gapped over her breasts. 'Happy New Year!' she shouted at them.

'Not yet,' Mags said.

'One!' everyone else yelled.

'Happy New Year,' Noel said to Natalie.

Then Natalie leaned toward him, and he leaned toward her, and they kissed.

31 December 2013, almost midnight

Noel was standing on the arm of the couch with his hands out to Mags.

Mags was walking past him, shaking her head.

'Come on!' he shouted over the music.

She shook her head *and* rolled her eyes.

'It's our last chance to dance together!' he said. 'It's our senior year!'

'We have months left to dance,' Mags said, stopping at the food table to get a mini quiche.

Noel walked down the couch, stepped onto the coffee table, then stretched one long leg out as far as he could to make it onto the love seat next to Mags.

'They're playing our song,' he said.

'They're playing "Baby Got Back," ' Mags said.

Noel grinned.

'Just for that,' she said, 'I'm never dancing with you.'

'You never dance with me anyway,' he said.

'I do everything else with you,' Mags whined. It was true. She studied with Noel. She ate lunch with Noel. She picked Noel up on the way to school. 'I even go with you to get a haircut.'

He touched the back of his hair. It was brown and thick, and fell in loose curls down to his collar. 'Mags, when you don't go, they cut it too short.'

'I'm not complaining,' she said. 'I'm just sitting this round out.'

'What're you eating?' he asked.

Mags looked down at the tray. 'Some kind of quiche, I think.'

'Can I eat it?'

She popped another one in her mouth and mushed it around. It didn't taste like tree nuts or strawberries or kiwi fruit or shellfish. 'I think so,' she said. She held up a quiche, and Noel leaned over and ate it out of her fingers. Standing on the love seat, he was seven-and-a-half feet tall. He was wearing a ridiculous white suit. Three pieces. Where did somebody even find a three-piece white suit?

'S'good,' he said. 'Thanks.' He reached for Mags's Coke, and she let him have it—then he jerked it away from his mouth and cocked his head. 'Margaret. They're playing our song.'

Mags listened. 'Is this that Ke$ha song?'

'Dance with me. It's our anniversary.'

'I don't like dancing with a bunch of people.'

'But that's the best way to dance! Dancing is a communal experience!'

'For you,' Mags said, pushing his thigh. He wavered, but didn't fall. 'We're not the same person.'

'I know,' Noel said with a sigh. '*You* can eat

tree nuts. Eat one of those brownies for me—let me watch.'

Mags looked at the buffet and pointed to a plate of pecan brownies. 'These?'

'Yeah,' Noel said.

She picked up a brownie and took a bite. Crumbs fell on her flowered dress, and she brushed them off.

'Is it good?' he asked.

'Really good,' she said. 'Really dense. Moist.' She took another bite.

'So unfair,' Noel said, holding on to the back of the love seat and leaning farther over. 'Let me see.'

Mags opened her mouth and stuck out her tongue.

'Unfair,' he said. 'That looks delicious.'

She closed her mouth and nodded.

'Finish your delicious brownie and dance with me,' he said.

'The whole world is dancing with you,' Mags said. 'Leave me alone.'

She grabbed another quiche and another brownie, then put Noel behind her.

There weren't that many places to sit in Alicia's basement; that's why Mags usually ended up on the floor. (And maybe why Noel usually ended up on the coffee table.) Pony had claimed the beanbag by the bar in the corner, and Simini was sitting on his lap. Simini smiled at Mags, and Mags smiled back and waved.

There wasn't any booze in the bar. Alicia's parents put it away whenever she had a party. All the barstools were taken, so Mags got a hand from somebody and sat up on the bar itself.

She watched Noel dance. (With Natalie. And then with Alicia and Connor. And then by himself, with his arms over his head.)

She watched everybody dance.

They had all their parties in this basement. After football games and after dances. Two years ago, Mags hadn't really known anybody in this room,

except for Alicia. Now everybody here was either a best friend, or a friend, or someone she knew well enough to stay away from . . .

Or Noel.

Mags finished her brownie and watched Noel jump around.

Noel was her very best friend—even if she wasn't his. Noel was her *person*.

He was the first person she talked to in the morning, and the last person she texted at night. Not intentionally or methodically. That's just the way it was between them. If she didn't tell Noel about something, it was almost like it didn't happen.

They'd been tight ever since they ended up in journalism class together, the second semester of sophomore year. (*That's* when they should celebrate their friendiversary—not on New Year's Eve.) And then they signed up for photography and tennis together.

They were so tight, Mags went with Noel to prom last year, even though he already had a date.

'Obviously, you're coming with us,' Noel said.

'Is that okay with Amy?'

'Amy knows we're a package deal. She probably

wouldn't even like me if I wasn't standing right next to you.'

(Noel and Amy never went out again after prom. They weren't together long enough to break up.)

Mags was thinking about getting another brownie when someone suddenly turned off the music, and someone else flickered the lights. Alicia ran by the bar, shouting, 'It's almost midnight!'

'Ten!' Pony called out a few seconds later.

Mags glanced around the room until she found Noel again—standing on the couch. He was already looking at her. He stepped onto the coffee table in Mags's direction and grinned, wolfishly. All of Noel's grins were a little bit wolfish: he had way too many teeth. Mags took a breath that shook on the way out. (Noel was her *person.*)

'Eight!' the room shouted.

Noel beckoned her with his hand.

Mags raised an eyebrow.

He waved at her again and made a face that said, *Come on, Mags.*

'Four!'

Then Frankie stepped onto the coffee table with Noel and slung an arm around his shoulders.

'Three!'

Noel turned to Frankie and grinned.

'Two!'

Frankie raised her eyebrows.

'One!'

Frankie leaned up into Noel. And Noel leaned down into Frankie.

And they kissed.

31 December 2014, about nine p.m.

Mags hadn't seen Noel yet this winter break. His family went to Walt Disney World for Christmas.

It's 80 degrees, he texted her, *and I've been wearing mouse ears for 72 hours straight.*

Mags hadn't seen Noel since August, when she went over to his house early one morning to say good-bye before his dad drove him to Notre Dame.

Noel didn't come home for Thanksgiving; plane tickets were too expensive.

She'd seen photos he posted of other people online. (People from his residence hall. People at parties. Girls.) And she and Noel had texted. They'd texted a lot. But Mags hadn't seen him since August—she hadn't heard his voice since then.

Honestly, she couldn't remember it. She couldn't remember ever thinking about Noel's voice before. Whether it was deep and rumbled. Or high and smooth. She couldn't remember what Noel sounded like—or what he looked like, not in motion. She could only see his face in the dozens of photos she still had saved on her phone.

You're going to Alicia's, yeah? he'd texted her yesterday. He was in an airport, on his way home.

Where else would I go? Mags texted back.

Cool.

Mags got to Alicia's early and helped her clean out the basement, then helped Alicia's mom frost the brownies. Alicia was home from college in South Dakota; she had a tattoo on her back now of a meadowlark.

Mags didn't have any new tattoos. She hadn't changed at all. She hadn't even left Omaha—she got a scholarship to study industrial design at one of the

schools in town. A full scholarship. It would have been stupid for Mags to leave.

Nobody showed up for the party on time, but everybody showed up.

'Is Noel coming?' Alicia asked, when the doorbell had stopped ringing.

How would I know? Mags wanted to say. But she did know. 'Yeah, he's coming,' she said. 'He'll be here.' She'd gotten a little chocolate on the sleeve of her dress. She tried to scrape it off with her fingernail.

Mags had changed three times before she settled on this dress.

She was going to wear a dress that Noel had always liked, gray with deep red peonies—but she didn't want him to think that she hadn't had a single original thought since the last time she saw him.

So she'd changed. Then changed again. And ended up in this one, a cream-colored lace shift that she'd never worn before, with baroque-patterned pink and gold tights.

She stood in front of her bedroom mirror, staring at herself. At her dark brown hair. Her thick eyebrows and blunt chin. She tried to see herself the way Noel would see her, for the first time since August. Then she tried to pretend she didn't care.

Then she left.

She got halfway to her car, then ran back up to her room to put on the earrings Noel had given her last year for her eighteenth birthday—angel wings.

Mags was talking to Pony when Noel finally arrived. Pony was in school in Iowa, studying engineering. He'd grown his hair back out into a ponytail, and Simini was tugging on it just because it made her happy. She was studying art in Utah, but she was probably going to transfer to Iowa. Or Pony was going to move to Utah. Or they were going to meet in the middle. 'What's in the middle?' Pony said. 'Nebraska? Shit, honey, maybe we should move home.'

Mags felt it when Noel walked in. (He came in through the back door, and a bunch of cold air came in with him.)

She looked up over Pony's shoulder and saw Noel, and Noel saw her—and he strode straight through the basement, over the love seat and up onto the coffee table and over the couch and through Pony and Simini, and wrapped his arms around Mags, swinging her in a circle.

'Mags!' Noel said.

HAPPY NE

'Noel,' Mags whispered.

Noel hugged Pony and Simini, too. And Frankie and Alicia and Connor. And everybody. Noel was a hugger.

Then he came back to Mags and pinned her against the wall, crowding her as much as hugging her. 'Oh, God, Mags,' he said. 'Never leave me.'

'I never left you,' she said to his chest. 'I never go anywhere.'

'Never let me leave you,' he said to the top of her head.

'When do you go back to Notre Dame?' she asked.

'Sunday.'

Noel was wearing wine-colored pants (softer than jeans, rougher than velvet), a blue-on-blue striped T-shirt, and a gray jacket with the collar turned up.

He was as pale as ever.

His eyes were as wide and as blue.

But his hair was cut short: buzzed over his ears and up the back, with long brown curls spilling out over his forehead. Mags brought her hand up to the back of his head. It felt like something was missing.

'You should have come with me, Margaret,' he said. 'The young woman who attacked me couldn't stop herself.'

'No,' she said, rubbing Noel's scalp. 'It looks good. It suits you.'

Everything was the same, and everything was different.

Same people. Same music. Same couches.

But they'd all grown apart for four months, and in wildly different directions.

Frankie brought beer and hid it under the couch, and Natalie was drunk when she got there. Connor brought his new college boyfriend, and everyone hated him—and Alicia kept trying to pull Connor aside to tell him so. The basement seemed more crowded than usual, and there wasn't as much dancing. . . .

There was about as much dancing as there would be at a normal party—at somebody else's party. *Their* parties used to be *different*. They used to be twenty-five people in a basement who knew each other so well, they never had to hold back.

Noel didn't dance tonight. He stuck with Pony and Simini and Frankie. He stuck by Mags's side, like he was glued there.

She was so glad that she and Noel hadn't stopped texting—that she still knew what he woke up worried about. Everybody else's inside jokes were seven months old, but Noel and Mags hadn't missed a beat.

Noel took a beer when Frankie offered him one. But when Mags rolled her eyes, he handed it to Pony.

'Is it weird being in Omaha?' Simini asked her. 'Now that everybody's left?'

'It's like walking through the mall after it closes,' Mags said. 'I miss you guys so much.'

Noel startled. 'Hey,' he said to Mags, pulling on her sleeve.

'What?'

'Come here, come here—come with me.'

He was pulling her away from their friends, out of the basement, up the stairs. When they got to the first floor, he said, 'Too far, can't hear the music.'

'What?'

They went down the stairs again and stopped midway, and Noel switched places with her, so she was standing on the higher step. 'Dance with me, Mags, they're playing our song.'

Mags tipped her head. '"A Thousand Years"?'

'It's our actual song,' he said. 'Dance with me.'

'How is this our song?' she asked.

'It was playing when we met,' Noel said.

'When?'

'When we met,' he said, rolling his hand, like he was hurrying her along.

'When we met *here*?'

'Yes. When we met. Downstairs. Sophomore year. And you saved my life.'

'I never saved your life, Noel.'

'Why do you always ruin this story?'

'You remember the song that was playing when we met?'

'I always remember the song that's playing,' he said. 'All the time.'

That was true, he did. All Mags could think to say now was, 'What?'

Noel groaned.

'I don't like to dance,' she said.

'You don't like to dance *in front of people*,' he said.

'That's true.'

'Just a minute.' Noel sighed and ran downstairs. 'Don't go anywhere,' he shouted up to her.

'I never go anywhere!' she shouted back.

She heard the song start over.

Then Noel was running back up the stairs. He stood on the step below her and held up his hands. 'Please.'

Mags sighed and lifted up her hands. She wasn't sure what to do with them . . .

Noel took one of her hands in his and put her other hand on his shoulder, curling his arm around her waist. 'Jesus Christ,' he said, 'was that so hard?'

'I don't know why this is so important to you,' she said. 'Dancing.'

'I don't know why it's so important to you,' he said. 'Not to dance with me.'

She was a little bit taller than him like this. They were swaying.

Alicia's mom came down the stairs. 'Hey, Mags. Hey, Noel—how's Notre Dame?'

Noel pulled Mags closer to let Mrs. Porter squeeze by. 'Good,' he said.

'You guys really fell asleep against Michigan.'

'I'm not actually on the football team,' Noel said.

'That's no excuse,' Mrs. Porter said.

Noel didn't loosen his grip after Alicia's mom

was past them. His arm was all the way around Mags's waist now, and their stomachs and chests were pressed together.

They'd touched a lot, over the years, as friends. Noel liked to touch. Noel hugged. And tickled and pulled hair. Noel pulled people into his lap. He apparently kissed anyone who raised their eyebrows at him on New Year's Eve. . . .

But Noel had never held Mags like this.

Mags had never felt his belt buckle in her hip. She'd never tasted his breath.

Mrs. Porter came back up the stairs, and Noel held Mags even tighter.

'A Thousand Years' began again.

'Did you tell somebody to start it over?' Mags asked.

'I put it on repeat,' he said. 'They'll stop it when they notice.'

'Was this on the *Twilight* sound track?'

'Dance with me, Mags.'

'I am,' she said.

'I know,' he said. 'Don't stop.'

'Okay.' Mags had been holding herself rigid, so that she'd still be standing upright, even if Noel let go. She stopped that now. She relaxed into his

grip and let her arm slide over his shoulder. She touched the back of his hair again because she wanted to—because it was still missing.

'You don't like it,' he said.

'I do like it,' she said. 'It's different.'

'You're different.'

Mags made a face that said, *You're crazy*.

'You are,' Noel said.

'I'm exactly the same,' she said. 'I'm the only one who's the same.'

'You're the most different.'

'How?'

'I don't know,' he said. 'It's like we all left, and you let go—and *you're* the one who drifted away.'

'That's bananas,' Mags said. 'I talk to you every day.'

'It's not enough,' he said. 'I've never seen this dress before.'

'You don't like my dress?'

'No.' Noel shook his head. She wasn't used to seeing him like this. Agitated. 'I like it. It's pretty. But it's different. You're different. I feel like I can't get close enough to you.' He pushed his forehead into hers.

She pushed back. 'We're pretty close, Noel.'

He sighed, frustrated, and it filled her nose and mouth. 'Why don't you have a boyfriend?'

Mags frowned. 'Maybe I do.'

He looked devastated and pulled his head back. 'You wouldn't tell me something like that?'

'No,' she said, 'no—Noel, of course, I would. I'd tell you. I just don't know what you want me to say. I don't know why I don't have a boyfriend.'

'It's going to get worse,' he said. 'You're going to keep changing.'

'Well, so are you,' she said.

'I never change.'

Mags laughed. 'You're a kaleidoscope. You change every time I look away.'

'Don't you hate that?' he asked.

Mags shook her head. Her nose rubbed against his. 'I love it.'

They'd stopped swaying.

'Are we still dancing?' she asked.

'We're still dancing. Don't get any big ideas, Margaret.' He let go of her hand and wrapped that arm around her, too. 'Don't go anywhere.'

'I never go anywhere,' Mags whispered.

He shook his head like she was a liar. 'You're my *best* friend,' he said.

'You have lots of best friends,' she said.

'No,' Noel said. 'Just you.'

Mags held on to his neck with both arms. She pushed on his forehead. He smelled like skin.

'I can't get close enough,' Noel said.

*

Somebody realized that the song was on repeat and skipped to the next one.

Somebody else realized that Mags and Noel were gone. Natalie came looking for Noel. 'Noel! Come dance with me! They're playing our song!'

It was that Ke$ha song.

Noel pulled away from Mags. He grinned at her sheepishly. Like he'd been silly on the stairway, but she'd forgive him, wouldn't she? And there was a party downstairs, they should be at the party, right?

Noel went downstairs, and Mags followed.

The party had changed while they were gone: Everybody seemed a little bit younger again. They'd kicked off their shoes and were jumping on couches. They were singing all the words to the songs they always sang all the words to.

Noel took off his jacket and threw it to Mags. She caught it because she had good hands.

Noel looked good.

Long and pale. In dark red jeans that no one else would wear. In a T-shirt that would have hung on him last year.

He looked so good.

And she loved him so much.

And Mags couldn't do it again.

She couldn't stand across the room and watch Noel kiss someone else. Not tonight. She couldn't watch somebody else get the kiss she'd been working so hard for, since the moment they'd met.

So, a few minutes before midnight, Mags scooped up a handful of Chex mix and acted like she was going into the hall. Like maybe she was going to the bathroom. Or maybe she was going to check the filter on the furnace.

Then she slipped out the back door. No one would think to look for her outside in the snow.

It was cold, but Mags still had Noel's jacket, so she put it on. She leaned against the foundation of Alicia's house and ate Alicia's mom's Chex mix—Mrs. Porter made the best Chex mix—and listened to the music.

Then the music stopped, and the counting started.

And it was *good* that Mags was out here, because it would hurt too much to be in there. It always hurt too much, and this year, it might kill her.

'Seven!'

'Six!'

'Mags?' someone called.

It was Noel. She recognized his voice.

'Margaret?'

'Four!'

'Here,' Mags said. Then, a little louder, 'Here!' Because she was his best friend, and avoiding him was one thing, but hiding from him was another.

'Two!'

'Mags . . .'

She could see Noel then, in a shaft of moonlight breaking through the slats of the deck above her. His eyes had gone all soft, and he was raising his eyebrows.

'One!'

Mags nodded, and pushed with her shoulders away from the house, then Noel pushed her right back—pinning her as much as he was hugging her as much as he was crowding her against the wall.

He kissed her hard.

Mags hooked both arms around the back of his head, pressing their faces together, their chins and open mouths.

Noel held on to both of her shoulders.

After a few minutes—maybe more than a few

minutes, after awhile—they both seemed to trust the other not to go.

They eased up.

Mags petted Noel's curls, pushing them out of his face. Noel pinned her to the wall from his hips to his shoulders, kissing her to the rhythm of whatever song was playing inside now.

When he pulled away, she was going to tell him that she loved him; when he pulled away, she was going to tell him not to let go. 'Don't,' Mags said, when Noel finally lifted his head.

'Mags,' he whispered. 'My lips are going numb.'

'Then don't kiss,' she said. 'But don't go.'

'No . . .' Noel pushed away from her, and her whole front went cold. 'My lips are going numb—were you eating strawberries?'

'Oh, God,' she said. 'Chex mix.'

'Chex mix?'

'Cashews,' she said. 'And probably other tree nuts.'

'Ah,' Noel said.

Mags was already dragging him away from the wall. 'Do you have something with you?'

'Benadryl,' he said. 'In my car. But it makes me sleepy. I'm probably fine.'

'Where are your keys?'

'In my pocket,' he said, pointing at her, at his jacket. His tongue sounded thick.

Mags found the keys and kept pulling him. His car was parked on the street, and the Benadryl was in the glove compartment. Mags watched Noel take it, then stood with her arms folded, waiting for whatever came next.

'Can you breathe?' she asked.

'I can breathe.'

'What usually happens?'

He grinned. 'This has never happened before.'

'You know what I mean.'

'My mouth tingles. My tongue and lips swell up. I get hives. Do you want to check me for hives?' Wolfish.

'Then what?' she asked.

'Then nothing,' he said. 'Then I take Benadryl. I have an EpiPen, but I've never had to use it.'

'I'm going to check you for hives,' she said.

He grinned again and held out his arms. She looked at them. She lifted up his striped T-shirt. . . . He was pale. And covered in goose bumps. And there were freckles she'd never known about on his chest.

'I don't think you have hives,' she said.

'I can feel the Benadryl working already.' He dropped his arms and put them around her.

'Don't kiss me again,' Mags said.

'Immediately,' Noel said. 'I won't kiss you again immediately.'

She leaned into him, her temple on his chin, and closed her eyes.

'I knew you'd save my life,' he said.

'I wouldn't have had to save it if I didn't almost kill you.'

'Don't give yourself too much credit. It's the tree nuts who are trying to kill me.'

She nodded.

They were both quiet for a few minutes.

'Noel?'

'Yeah?'

She had to ask him this—she had to make herself ask it: 'Are you just being melodramatic?'

'Mags, I promise. I wouldn't fake an allergic response.'

'No,' she said. 'With the kiss.'

'There was more than one kiss. . . .'

'With all of them,' she said. 'Were you just—embellishing?'

Mags braced for him to say something silly.

'No,' Noel said. Then, 'Were you just humoring me?

'God. No,' she said. 'Did it feel like I was humoring you?'

Noel shook his head, rubbing his chin into her temple.

'What are we doing?' Mags asked.

'I don't know. . . .' he said eventually. 'I know things have to change, but . . . I can't lose you. I don't think I get another one like you.'

'I'm not going anywhere, Noel.'

'You *are,'* he said, squeezing her. 'And it's okay. Just . . . I need you to take me with you.'

Mags didn't know what to say to that.

It was cold. Noel was shivering. She should give him his jacket.

'Mags?'

'Yeah?'

'What do *you* need?'

Mags swallowed.

In the three years she and Noel had been friends, she'd spent a lot of time pretending she didn't need anything more than what he was already giving her. She'd told herself there was a difference

between wanting something and needing it. . . .

'I need you to be my person,' Mags said. 'I need to see you. And hear you. I need you to stay alive. And I need you to stop kissing other people just because they're standing next to you when the ball drops.'

Noel laughed.

'I also need you not to laugh at me,' she said.

He pulled his face back and looked at her. 'No, you don't.'

She kissed his chin without opening her mouth.

'You can have all those things,' he said carefully. 'You can have me, Mags, if you want me.'

'I've always wanted you,' she said, mortified by the extent to which it was true.

Noel leaned in to kiss her, and she dropped her forehead against his lips.

They were quiet.

And it was cold.

'Happy anniversary, Mags.'

'Happy New Year, Noel.'

KINDRED SPIRITS

Monday 14 December 2015

There were already two people sitting outside [illegible]

Monday 14 December 2015

There were already two people sitting outside the theater when Elena got there, so she wouldn't be first in line. But that was OK. She was still here—she was still *doing this*.

She grabbed her sleeping bag, and the backpack she'd stocked with books and food and anti-bacterial wipes, and got out of the car as quickly as possible; it looked like her mom might make one last attempt to talk Elena out of this.

She rolled down her window to frown at Elena directly. 'I don't see a Portaloo.'

Elena had said there would be a Portaloo. 'I'll figure it out,' Elena said quietly. 'These guys are figuring it out.'

'They're men,' her mom said. 'They can pee anywhere.'

'I'll hold it,' Elena said.

'For four days?'

'Mom,' Elena said. And what she meant was: *We've*

been through this. We've talked about it for weeks and weeks. I know you don't approve. But I'm still doing it.

Elena dropped her gear on the sidewalk, behind a tall white boy who was second in line. 'OK,' she said cheerfully to her mom. 'I've got this. See you Thursday!'

Her mom was still frowning. 'See you after lunch,' she said, then rolled up her window and drove away.

Elena turned back to the line, smiling her best first-day-of-school smile. The guy next to her—he looked like he was probably about her age, seventeen or eighteen—didn't look up. First in line was a big white guy with a blond beard. He looked old enough to be one of Elena's teachers, and he was sitting in a fold-out camping chair with his feet propped up on a giant cooler. 'Hey!' he said happily. 'Welcome to Star Wars, man! Welcome to the line!'

This, she quickly learned, was Troy. He'd been in line since Thursday morning. 'I wanted to invest at least a week in this, you know? I really wanted to gather my focus.'

The younger guy, Gabe, had got in line Thursday night.

'There was a couple who hung out with us Saturday for a few hours,' Troy said, 'but one of them forgot her sunglasses, so they went home. Weak!'

Elena hadn't brought any sunglasses. She squinted into the sun.

'I'm guessing this is your first line,' Troy said.

'How can you tell?' she asked.

'I can tell,' he said, chuckling. 'I can always tell. It's Gabe's first line, too.'

'We were eight when the last Star Wars movie came out,' Gabe said, not looking up from his book.

'*Revenge of the Sith*!' Troy said. 'That wasn't much of a line anyway. It was no *Empire*.'

'Nothing is,' Elena said.

Troy's face got somber. 'Hear, hear, Elena. Hear, hear.'

All right, so . . . she'd expected there to be more people here.

The Facebook group she'd found—Camp Star Wars: Omaha!!!—had eighty-five members, not including Elena, who was more of a lurker than a joiner. This was definitely the right theater; the Facebook posts had been very clear. (Maybe it was Troy who posted them.)

Elena had planned to continue her more-lurker-than-joiner strategy in the line. She thought she'd show up and then sort of disappear into the crowd until she got her sea legs. Her line legs. It was a pretty good strategy for most social situations: show up, fall back, let somebody else break the ice and take the spotlight. Somebody else always would. Extroverts were nothing if not dependable.

But even an expert mid-trovert like Elena couldn't lie low in a crowd of three. (Though this Gabe kid seemed to be trying.) Elena was going to be here for four days. She was going to have to *talk* to these people, at least until someone else showed up.

'Cold enough for you?' Troy asked.

'Actually I think I might be little overdressed,' Elena said.

She was wearing three layers on the bottom and four on top, and she had a big puffy coat if she needed it. If the temperature dropped dangerously low—which would be inevitable during a normal Omaha December—she'd have to go home. But the forecast was pretty mild. (Thanks, global warming?)

'What were they thinking when they scheduled this movie for December?' Troy said. 'They weren't thinking of us, I can tell you. *May*,' he said, shaking his head. 'May is when you release a Star Wars movie. If this movie were a May movie, the line would already be around the block.'

'Lucky for us, I guess,' Elena said. 'We get to be first.'

'Oh, I'd be first no matter what,' Troy said. 'I am here for it, you know?' He cupped his hands around his lips and shouted, 'I'm here for it!'

Me, too, Elena thought.

Elena couldn't remember the first time she saw a Star Wars movie . . . in the same way she couldn't remember the first time she saw her parents. Star Wars had just always *been* there. There was a stuffed Chewbacca in her crib.

The original trilogy were her dad's favorite movies—he practically knew them by heart—so when Elena was little, like four or five, she'd say they were her favorite movies, too. Because she wanted to be just like him.

And then, as she got older, the movies started to actually sink in. Like, they went from something

Elena could recite to something she could *feel*. She made them her own. And then she'd kept making them her own. However Elena changed or grew, Star Wars seemed to be there for her in a new way.

When she'd found out that there were going to be sequels—*real* sequels, Han and Leia and Luke sequels—she'd flipped out. That's when she'd decided to get in line.

She didn't want to miss this moment. Not just this moment in the world, but this moment *in her life*.

If you broke Elena's heart, Star Wars would spill out. This was a holy day for her—it was a cosmic event. This was her planets lining up. (*Tatooine, Coruscant, Hoth.)*

And Elena was going to be here for it.

Her left foot was asleep.

She kept kicking the sidewalk, then stood up to bounce.

'Is your leg asleep again?' Troy said. 'I'm worried about your circulation.'

'It's fine,' Elena said, stamping her foot.

She'd only been sitting for two hours, but she was so bored she could hardly stand it. She could literally hardly stand; even her blood vessels were bored.

She'd brought lots of books. (She'd planned to read Star Wars books whenever she had a quiet moment in line.) (Which was every moment so far.) But the wind kept blowing the pages, and the paper was so bright in the sun that reading made her eyes water.

None of that seemed to bother silent Gabe, who read his paperback without seeming to notice the sun, the traffic, Troy, Elena or Elena's mom, who kept driving by slowly, like someone trying to buy drugs.

'The Imperial March' started playing, and Elena answered her phone.

'Why don't I pick you up now?' her mom said. 'Then you can get back in line when there are more girls here.'

'I'm fine,' Elena said.

'You don't even know these men. They could be sexual predators.'

'This doesn't seem like a very good place to prey,' Elena whispered, glancing over at Gabe, who was still absorbed in his book. He was pale with curly, milk-chocolate-colored hair and

rosy cheeks. He looked like Clark Kent's skinny cousin.

'You know you have to be extra careful,' her mom said. 'You look so young.'

'We've been through this,' Elena said.

They'd been through it a lot:

'*You look twelve,*' her mom would say.

And Elena couldn't really argue. She was short and small. She could shop in the kids section. And the fact that she was Vietnamese seemed to scramble non-Asians' perceptions of her. She was always being mistaken for a kid.

But what was she supposed to do about that? Act like a kid until she looked like an adult? Start smoking and spend too much time in the sun?

'*Just because I look twelve doesn't mean you can treat me like I'm twelve,*' Elena would say. '*I'm going to college next year.*'

'You told me there'd be other girls here,' her mom said.

'There will be.'

'Good. I'll bring you back after they get here.'

'I've gotta go,' Elena said. 'I'm trying to conserve my phone battery.'

'Elena—'

'I've got to go!' Elena hung up.

The first theater employees started showing up around two. One, who looked like the manager—a Latino guy in his thirties, wearing maroon pants and a matching tie—stopped in front of the line and crossed his arms.

'So we've got a new addition, huh?'

Elena smiled.

He didn't smile back. 'You know you can buy your ticket online, right?'

'I already bought my ticket,' Elena said.

'Then you're guaranteed a seat. You don't have to wait in line.'

'Um,' Elena said. 'That's OK.'

'You can't talk her out of this,' Troy said. 'She's a true believer.'

'I'm not trying to talk anybody out of

anything,' the manager said, looking harried. 'I'm just explaining that this is an unnecessary gesture.'

'All the best ones are,' Troy said. 'Now open the doors. My bladder is about explode.'

The manager sighed. 'I don't have to let you use the restroom, you know.'

'Give it up, Mark,' Troy said. 'They tried that during *Phantom Menace*, and it didn't work then either.'

'I should make you hoof it to Starbucks,' the manager said, walking towards the front doors and unlocking them.

Troy stood up and made a big show of stretching. 'We take turns,' he said to Elena, 'in line order.'

She nodded.

The manager, Mark, held the door for Troy, but he was still looking at Elena. 'Do your parents know you're here?'

'I'm eighteen,' she said.

He looked surprised. 'Well, all right. Then I guess you're old enough to waste your own time.'

Elena was hoping Gabe would open up a little while Troy was gone. They'd been sitting next to each other for hours now, and he'd only said a few words. She thought maybe he was being so quiet because he didn't want to get Troy going on one of his stories. (Troy had *so* many stories—he'd camped out for every Star Wars opening since *The Empire Strikes Back*—and he was clearly pleased to have a captive audience.)

But Gabe, with his navy-blue peacoat and his gunmetal glasses, just sat there reading about the history of polio and ignoring her.

When Troy came out with an extra-large sack of popcorn, Gabe nodded at Elena. 'Go ahead.'

'I'm fine,' Elena said. 'I just got here.' She wasn't fine; she had to pee so bad she was worried she was going to leak when she stood up.

Gabe didn't move. So Elena got up and walked into the theater. The manager kept an eye on her the whole time, like she might sneak in to see a movie. She should. It was so *warm* inside the theater.

When she got back outside, Gabe took his turn.

'We have to save his spot,' Troy said, 'and look out for his things as if they were our own. Code of the Line.' He held his bag of popcorn out over Gabe's sleeping bag.

Elena took some. 'What invalidates the code?' she asked.

'What do you mean?'

'Like, are there any circumstances where someone loses their spot?'

'That is a fine question,' he said. 'I mean, some things are obvious. If someone takes off, without telling anyone or leaving any collateral—they're out. I think there's a time limit, too. Like, you can't just go home and take a nap and expect to come back to your spot. Everybody else is here, earning it, you know? You don't get a free pass for that. Though there are always exceptions . . .'

'There are?'

'We're human. We had a guy in the *Phantom Menace* line who had to leave for therapy. We saved his place. But another guy tried to go to work, he said he was going to lose his job . . . We pushed his tent out of line.'

'You did?' Popcorn fell out of Elena's mouth. She picked it up. 'That's *brutal*.'

'No—' Troy was grave—'that's life. We were all going to lose our jobs. I camped out for three weeks. You think I got three weeks' vacation? At the zoo?'

'You worked at the zoo?'

'You've got to sacrifice something for this experience,' Troy said, refusing to be sidetracked.

'That's why we're here. You've got to leave some blood on the altar. I mean, you heard Mark. If you just want to see the new Star Wars movie, you can buy your ticket online and then forget about it until show time. But if you want to wait in line, you *wait in line*, you know?'

Elena was nodding. Gabe was standing on the sidewalk. 'Did you just vote me out of the line?' he asked.

Troy laughed. 'No, dude, you're good—you want some popcorn?'

Gabe took some and sat down.

Elena had been imagining this day for months. She'd been planning it for weeks.

This wasn't what she was expecting from the line experience.

This was more like being in an elevator with two random people. Like being *stuck* in an elevator.

Elena had been expecting . . . Well, more people, obviously. And more of a party. A celebration!

She'd thought it would be like all those photos she'd seen when she was a kid and the last Star Wars movies came out. All those fans out on the street, in communion with each other.

Elena had been too young to camp out then. Her dad wouldn't even let her *see* the prequels. He said she was too young. And then, when she grew up, he said they were too terrible. '*They'll just corrupt your love of Star Wars,*' he said. '*I wish I could unsee them.*'

So even though Star Wars was Elena's whole life at ten, she didn't get to go to the party.

She was eighteen now. She could do whatever she wanted. *So where was the party?*

The afternoon was even more mind-numbing than the morning.

Her mom drove by three or four more times. Elena pretended not to notice. She read a few chapters of a Star Wars book. Troy pointed out that all the expanded-universe books weren't canon any more—'Disney erased them from the timeline.' Elena said she didn't care, that she liked them anyway.

At nightfall, people started showing up for the evening movies, and Troy got into a fight with Mark about refilling his popcorn. 'It says, "*Endless refills same day only*,"' Troy said.

'You're perverting the intent,' Mark said.

Elena kept hoping that some of the people walking towards the theater were there to join the line—there were two thirty-something guys in Star Wars shirts who looked like good candidates, and a few college girls who looked nerdy enough—but they all walked right by.

Elena had stripped down to her Princess Leia T-shirt, but now that the sun was gone, she started reapplying her layers.

Maybe her mom was right. Maybe Elena should leave and come back when the line really got going . . .

What would Troy say? '*There was an Asian girl who hung out with us for a few hours; then her mom made her leave.*'

No, this was it. If Elena bailed, she couldn't come back.

She wrapped herself in her sleeping bag and pulled on a woolen hat with a big red pompom, taking a few more years off her appearance.

The fight with Mark seemed to leave Troy in a

funk. He put in earplugs and watched Netflix on his phone. Elena watched him hungrily—she was dying to use her phone. Her whole world was in there. Sitting outside in the cold and dark would be so much more bearable if she could read fanfiction or text her friends. But she only had one back-up battery pack to last four days . . . At least it was still bright enough to read. She was sitting just below a lit up Star Wars poster.

Her mom pulled up in front of the theater again at ten. Elena got up and walked to the car.

'I don't like this,' her mom said. 'People are going to think you're homeless.'

'No one will think that.'

'Homeless people are going to bother you.'

'Probably not.'

'I talked to Dì Janet and she says you can buy your movie ticket online.'

'That's not the point.'

'It's just that—' Her mom rubbed her temple. 'Elena, I think this is the dumbest thing you've ever done in your life.'

'That's a good thing, Mom. Think about how much worse it could be.'

Her mom frowned and handed her a warm

covered dish. 'You answer your texts tonight.'

'I will.'

Elena stepped away from the car.

'Don't worry about her!' Troy shouted from behind her. 'She's in good hands!'

Elena's mom looked aghast. But she still drove away.

'I'm sorry,' Troy said. 'Did I make that worse? I meant the hands of the line.'

'It's OK,' Elena said, finding her spot against the wall.

Mark the theater manager came out one more time to give them a last call for the bathroom and concessions, which was pretty decent of him.

Troy was asleep by eleven, stretched out on his chair with an inflatable pillow wedged between him and the wall. He'd wrapped himself in fleece blankets, tipped his head back, and that was it.

Elena had planned to roll out her sleeping bag and sleep lying down. But that was back when she'd imagined a few dozen campers. It was different with just three people, and she felt too exposed at the end of the line. If she fell asleep lying down, someone could just drag her away in the night, and

Troy and Gabe would never notice.

She didn't think she was afraid of Troy and Gabe themselves. Troy hadn't said anything pervy yet. Not even about Princess Leia. And Gabe seemed painstakingly uninterested in Elena.

Her mom didn't trust them, but her mom didn't trust any guys. She used to just have it in for white guys. ('*White guys are the worst. They rap 2 Live Crew lyrics at you and expect you to laugh.*') But ever since she and Elena's dad had separated four years ago, her mom had taken a stand against any and every man, especially where Elena was concerned. '*Learn from my mistakes,*' she said.

Learn what? Elena wondered. Avoid men? Avoid love? Avoid radiologists who buy movie-replica lightsabers?

Usually when her mom gave her warnings like this, Elena would just give her a thumbs up. Like, *No prob, Bob.*

Because it really wasn't a problem. Avoid men? Done! This had literally never been an issue for her. When other girls complained about how to deal with unwanted male attention, Elena wouldn't feel jealous exactly, but she would feel curious—how does one go about attracting such attention? And is it impossible to attract just some of it? Just a small, manageable amount? Or was attention from boys all or nothing, like a tap that, once you'd found it, you could never turn off?

Elena's teeth were starting to chatter, and it wasn't even that cold out. But the cold of the ground had crept through her sleeping bag, through her jeans, through her long underwear and tights, and settled into her bones.

'You've gotta put something under your sleeping bag,' Gabe said. 'Or get off the ground.'

She looked where his butt must be. He lifted the side of his sleeping bag up. He was sitting on cardboard, two or three pieces.

'Does that work?' she asked.

'It helps,' he said.

'Well, I don't have a spare box on me . . .'

Gabe sighed. 'Hold my spot.'

He got up and shuffled out of his sleeping bag, walking down the street and disappearing behind the building. When he came back, he was carrying a few cardboard boxes. Raisinets. Sour Patch Kids.

'You take mine,' he said.

'What?'

'Move up, unless you don't want to sit between

us. Troy's an excellent windbreak.'

Elena shuffled over to Gabe's pile of boxes, pulling her things with her. Gabe quickly made himself a new nest and settled down again.

'It does help,' Elena said. 'Thanks.'

She tested her instincts, to see if she felt any less safe sitting between these two strangers than on the end. No. She felt about the same. 'You just want *me* to have to listen to Troy's stories,' she whispered.

'We can switch back in the morning,' he said.

'Do you know him?' she asked. 'Troy?'

'I didn't know him before,' Gabe said, 'but I have been sitting next to him for four days . . .'

Gabe picked up his book.

'Thanks,' Elena said again.

Gabe didn't answer.

Tuesday 15 December 2015

It didn't seem like Elena had slept, but she must have. She woke up slumped over her backpack with a patch of cold saliva on her chin.

'Star Wars!' someone was shouting from a car driving by.

'Star Wars!' Troy shouted back, raising his fist.

Yes, Elena thought, *Star Wars.* That's what this experience needed: more Star Wars.

Elena was going to rally.

So this wasn't the jubilant, communal, public display of affection she'd been expecting—it could still be *something.* It could still be memorable. She'd make it memorable.

'What does the Code of the Line say about going to Starbucks?' she asked.

Troy answered: 'Totally acceptable as long as you bring back some for us.'

Elena walked the six blocks to Starbucks and hung out in the bathroom for a while, painting little Yodas on her cheeks. She

had the Starbucks barista write character names on their cups. Troy was Admiral Ackbar, Gabe was General Dodonna, and Elena was Mon Mothma.

When she got back to the line, she took out her phone and carefully took a selfie of herself with the guys behind her. Gabe wouldn't look at the camera, but Troy played along. '*Third in line!*' Elena posted on Instagram. Which sounded much better than '*Last in Line!*'

'I dig your face paint,' Troy said. 'I've got a costume, but I'm saving it for opening night.'

'Do you always wear a costume on opening night?' Elena asked.

'Oh yeah. Usually I camp in it.'

'I want to hear about your costumes,' Elena said.

'You mean opening-night costumes? Or all my Star Wars costumes, including Halloween and May the Fourth parties?'

'We want to hear about *all* of them,' she said, glancing over at Gabe. 'Right?'

Gabe was looking at her like she was out of her mind.

After they got through Troy's costumes, Elena quizzed him about highs and lows from past lines. Then she suggested they play Star Wars trivia, which she quickly realized wasn't a good idea, because she couldn't answer any questions about the prequels, and she didn't want Troy and Gabe to guess that she hadn't actually seen them.

Elena *could* have seen them by now. She could have watched all three prequels after her dad moved to Florida—but it still felt like she'd be betraying him. And even though her dad had betrayed her by leaving, she didn't feel like watching Star

Wars movies just to spite him. That seemed like it really *would* corrupt her love for Star Wars. '*A Jedi uses the Force for knowledge and defense, never for attack.*' (Yoda.)

Elena's mom drove by a few times that morning. Elena just waved and tried to look like she was having the time of her life.

Nobody new got in line.

The highlight of Tuesday afternoon was when a photographer from the newspaper came by to take their picture.

'I'm looking for the Star Wars line,' he said. He had an oversized camera with a long black lens.

'That's us!' Troy said.

'Oh.' He squinted at them. 'I thought there was supposed to be a real line, like with people in costume.'

'Come back on opening night,' Troy said. 'My Poe Dameron will knock your socks off.'

The photographer looked at Elena's cheeks. 'Is that Shrek?'

'It's Yoda,' Gabe snapped. 'For Christ's sake.'

In the end, the photographer shot a close-up of Troy holding a photo of himself waiting in a much more interesting line fifteen years ago.

It was a humiliating setback for them as individuals and for the line as a whole.

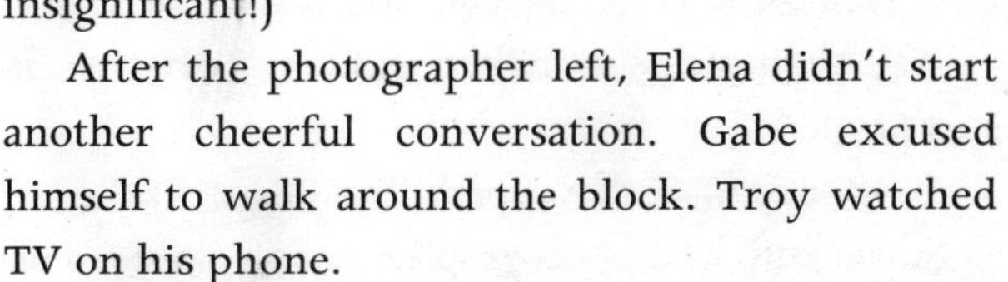

(Ugh. They weren't a *line*. They were just three cold nerds.) (They were three suckers who showed up for a party that didn't exist.) (They were statistically insignificant!)

After the photographer left, Elena didn't start another cheerful conversation. Gabe excused himself to walk around the block. Troy watched TV on his phone.

Elena took out her phone just long enough to take a photo of her flowered sneakers. '*My legs are permanently asleep,'* she posted. '*#LineProblems.'* Then she immediately put her phone away, before she could start wandering around online and enjoying herself.

When Gabe came back he was frowning more than Elena had ever seen a human being frown. Even her mother. It was the longest afternoon of her life.

By Tuesday evening, deep malaise had set in. Luke-staring-into-both-suns-of-Tatooine malaise.

Elena hid her face whenever movie-goers walked by. She only perked up when her mom came by around ten. *Gotta keep up appearances.*

When Elena stood up to go to the car, her whole body felt numb with cold and disuse. Her mom shoved a hot-water bottle out the window. 'Here.'

It was so hot that Elena dropped it. 'Thanks,' she said, picking it up.

'I don't think George Lucas would want you to do this,' her mom said.

'I didn't know you knew who George Lucas was.'

'Please. I was watching Star Wars movies before you were born. Your dad and I saw *Empire Strikes Back* five times in the theater.'

'Lucky,' Elena said.

'George Lucas is a father of daughters,' her mother said. 'He wouldn't want young girls freezing to death to prove their loyalty.'

'This isn't about George Lucas,' Elena said. 'He isn't even that involved in the sequels.'

'Come home,' her mom said. 'We'll watch *Empire Strikes Back* and I'll make hot cocoa.'

'I can't,' Elena said. 'I'll lose my place in line.'

'I think it will still be there for you in the morning.'

'Goodnight, Mom.'

Her mom sighed and held out a venti Starbucks cup. 'Stay warm. I'll leave my ringer on tonight in case you change your mind.'

Elena sat down with her coffee and tucked the hot-water bottle into her sleeping bag. It felt *amazing*.

'Call your Mom,' Gabe said flatly. 'I want to watch *Empire Strikes Back* and drink hot cocoa.'

She realized now that the coffee was a set-up.

It was two in the morning, and Elena was going to wet her pants. She looked up the line. Troy was wrapped in sleeping bags and a polar fleece, like a mummy. Gabe had pulled his knees up and tucked his head down a few hours ago.

Elena had been sleeping. Badly. She felt groggy and out of sorts and her bladder actually *hurt*. She kept fidgeting. Gabe lifted his head. 'What's wrong? Are you cold?'

'No,' Elena said. 'I mean, yes, of course. But no—I'm going to wet my pants.'

'Don't do that,' Gabe said.

'*I can't help it*. What am I supposed to do?'

'Go pee somewhere.'

'Where?'

'I don't know. Behind a car or something.'

'That's illegal!' Elena said. 'And gross!'

'Not as gross as peeing your pants.'

Elena closed her eyes. 'Ughhhhhhhhhh. Where have you guys been peeing?'

'Inside the theater,' he said.

'Don't you ever have to go at night?'

He shrugged. 'No.'

Elena felt tears rolling down her cheeks.

'Don't cry,' Gabe said. 'That won't help.'

She kept crying. It was going to happen soon.

'OK,' he said, standing up. 'Come on.'

'Where are we going?'

'To let you pee.'

'We can't leave without telling Troy,' she said. 'Code of the Line.'

'The Code of the Line also includes not soiling it. Come on.'

Troy had an extra-large Coke cup, and Gabe grabbed it. Elena got up, carefully, and followed him around to the back of the theater.

'OK,' he said, holding out the cup. 'You go behind the dumpster, pee in this cup, then put it in the dumpster.'

'What if there are cameras?' Elena said, taking the cup.

'I can't help you there. This isn't *Mission: Impossible*, you know?'

'But what if I need to pee more than this? I don't know how much I pee.'

'If your bladder held more than forty-four ounces, you wouldn't have to go to the bathroom constantly.'

She stood there, biting her lip.

'Elena.'

'Yeah?'

'You don't have any other options here. Pee in the cup.'

'Right,' she said. She walked, carefully, to the other side of the dumpster. 'I don't want you to listen!'

'Is this the first time you've peed around another human being?'

'Around a guy,' she shouted, 'yes!'

'I didn't ask for this!' Gabe shouted back. He started humming loudly—'The Imperial March'. It made Elena feel like her mom was coming.

She carefully peeled down her layers and hovered over the cup, trying not to touch it, and trying not to splash, still sort of crying. Gabe kept up the loud humming. When Elena was done, she put the lid on the cup and walked out. 'OK,' she said.

'Gross. You were supposed to throw it away.'

'I'm going to pour it down a storm drain! So it doesn't spill on anyone.'

'Whatever,' Gabe said.

When she'd disposed of the pee, and the cup, she sat back down next to him and dug in her bag for a wet wipe.

'I should just go home,' she said, scrubbing her hands.

'Do you have to pee again?'

'No.'

'Then why do you want to go home?'

'Well, obviously I'm not prepared for this!' She waved her arm around, encompassing the cold, the line, the trash can, the storm drain . . . 'And it isn't how I thought it was going to be.'

'How'd you think it was going to be?' Gabe asked.

'I don't know—*fun*.'

'You're camping on a sidewalk with strangers. Why would that be fun?'

'It always *looks* fun. In the pictures. Like, tent cities. And people meeting in line and making friends for life. Getting matching tattoos.'

'You want to get a matching tattoo with Troy?'

'You know what I mean.' She threw her wadded-up wet wipe on to the ground. 'I thought it was going to be a celebration, like a way to be really excited about Star Wars with a bunch of other people who are really excited about Star Wars. Like in Troy's stories. Like the time they all camped out for two weeks to see *Return of the Jedi* and ended up with soulmates and nicknames. The practical jokes that went on for days! The lightsaber battles!'

'You could still end up with a nickname,' Gabe said. 'Right now I'm thinking something to do with pee. Or cups.'

Elena wrapped her sleeping bag tighter.

'Good Old Pees-in-a-Cup,' Gabe said.

'Why are you here?' she asked. 'If you knew it was going to be miserable.'

'I'm here because I love Star Wars,' he said. 'Same as you.' He folded his arms on his knees and tucked his head down.

'But you don't even talk to me,' Elena said. 'To either of us.'

Gabe made a sarcastic noise, like *hrmph*.

'No, seriously,' she said. 'What's the point of getting in this line if you don't want to experience it with other people?'

'Maybe I just don't want to experience it with you,' he said. 'Have you thought of that?'

'Oh my God.' She scrunched up her face. '*No.* I haven't thought of that. Is that true? Why are you so mean?'

'It's not true,' he grumbled, lifting his head. 'I'm just tired. And I'm not—a people person. Sorry I'm not meeting your Star Wars dream line expectations.'

'Me, too.' She rubbed her hands together and blew in them.

'Why didn't your friends wait in line with you?' Gabe said. 'Then you could have had your party line.'

'None of my friends likes Star Wars.'

'Everybody likes Star Wars,' he said. 'Everybody likes everything these days. The whole world is a nerd.'

'Are you mad because other people like Star Wars? Are you mad because people *like me* like Star Wars?'

Gabe glowered at her. 'Maybe.'

'Well,' she said, 'my friends *do* like Star Wars. They're going to see it this weekend. But they don't like it like I do. They don't get a stomach ache about it.'

'Why does Star Wars give you a stomach ache?'

'I don't know. I just care about it so much.'

'I wasn't trying to call you a fake geek girl,' Gabe said.

'I didn't say that you were.'

'I mean, you obviously know the original trilogy inside out. And that's not even important, but you obviously do.'

'I've yet to determine whether you're a fake geek boy,' she said, pulling her sleeves down over her hands.

He laughed, and she was ninety per cent sure it wasn't sarcastic.

'Here's what bothers me,' he said, glowering slightly less, but still looking frustrated. 'I'm a nerd, right? Like obviously. Classic nerd. I hate sports. I know every Weird Al song by heart. I don't know how to talk to most people. I'm probably going to get a job in computer science. Like, I know those are all stereotypes, but they're also true of me. That's who I am. And the thing about nerd culture being mainstream culture now means that there's no place to just be a nerd among other nerds—without being reminded that you're the nerd. Do you follow me?'

'Only sort of,' Elena said.

'OK. So. If I go to a football party at my brother's house, I don't know anything about football, and I'm the nerd. And if I go dancing with my friend who likes to dance, well, I don't dance, and I don't like loud music, so I'm the nerd. But *now*, even if I go see a comic-book movie, the whole world is there—so I'm still the nerd. I would have thought that a *Star Wars line* would be safe,' he said, waving his arm around the way Elena had. 'No way am I going to feel like a social outcast in a Star Wars line. No way am I going to have to sit next to one of the *cool girls* for four days.'

'Whoa,' Elena said. 'I'm not a cool girl.'

'Give me a break.'

She held up her index finger. 'I feel like I need to say that everyone should be welcome in a Star Wars line, socially successful or not, but also, *whoa*. I am a nerd,' she said. 'That's what this was supposed to be, a chance to talk to people who wouldn't care that I'm awkward in literally every other situation.'

'That's not true,' he said, rolling his eyes.

'It is.'

'You have friends. You have a clique. You walk down the hall like you own the place.'

'You seem to have mistaken me for the movie *Mean Girls,*' Elena said. 'Also, are you saying you don't have friends at your school? Have you considered that maybe it's your silent pouting that drives people away?'

'I have friends,' Gabe said. 'That's not the point.'

'So you have *friends,* but you think I have a *clique.*'

'I'm pretty sure of it.'

'I feel like you're projecting your clearly problematic girl issues on me,' she said.

Gabe rolled his eyes again. 'I thought you said you couldn't talk to people,' he said. 'You don't seem to have any problems talking to me.'

'I'm having *a lot* of problems talking to you.'

'OK, then, let's stop.'

Was Gabe really mad? She couldn't tell.

Was Elena mad? She also couldn't tell . . .

Yes. *Yes,* Elena *was* mad. Who was Gabe to take her inventory like this? He didn't know her. And he was giving her zero benefit of the doubt; she'd been giving him nothing *but* benefit of the doubt for thirty-six hours.

'For what it's worth,' she said, without looking at him, 'I haven't thought, *Whoa, Gabe sure is a nerd*, even once since I sat down.'

He didn't say anything.

Elena squirmed. She wrapped her sleeping bag as tightly as she could and rearranged her legs. 'Uggggggggch.'

'I get it,' he said. 'You think I'm a jerk.'

'No. *Yes*, but no—I have to pee again.'

'You just went.'

'I know, I can't help it. Sometimes it happens in waves.'

'Can you wait?'

'*No*.'

Gabe sighed and stood up. 'Come on. Let's go back to the dumpster.'

'I threw away the cup!' Elena said.

'You still have your hot-water bottle—'

'*No*.'

Gabe clicked his tongue like he was thinking. Elena started rooting through her backpack. Everything she'd brought was in plastic bags.

'Aha!' Gabe said. He reached behind her sleeping

bag and pulled out her Starbucks cup. 'This is perfect,' he said. 'It's already got your name on it.'

They left their sleeping bags and shuffled to the back of the theater again. It was no less humiliating the second time around.

'You're definitely getting a nickname,' Gabe said when she sat down again.

Elena crawled into her sleeping bag, feeling more unbelievably tired than unbelievably uncomfortable, like maybe she'd be able to get some sleep for real now.

'I was born at the wrong time,' she said. 'And in the wrong climate. It should be 1983, and I should be sitting outside Mann's Chinese Theatre in Hollywood, California.'

'They're camping outside the Chinese Theatre tonight,' Gabe said. 'Troy says we're all one line.'

'I'm probably last in that one, too,' Elena said.

She rolled away from Gabe and fell asleep.

Wednesday 16 December 2015

'The Force awakens!' Troy shouted.

Elena pulled her hat down over her eyes.

'Come on, Elena,' Troy said. 'We're hoping you'll get coffee again.'

'Because I'm a woman?'

'No. Because you probably have to pee,' Gabe said.

Elena did. 'Fine, tell me what you want.'

Twenty minutes later she was staring at herself in the Starbucks mirror. She was starting to look like someone who slept on the street and washed up in Starbucks bathrooms.

There'd been an actual homeless person sitting outside the Starbucks when Elena walked in, and it made her feel like a big creep to think she was doing this for fun. (It wasn't even fun!)

She told the barista their names were 'Tarkin', 'Veers' and 'Ozzel'.

'Feeling your dark side today, huh?' Troy said when she handed him his cup.

'Pretty much,' Elena said, dropping to the ground. 'Fear, anger, hate, suffering . . .'

'T-minus one!' Troy said. 'One more day. *One more day!* I can't believe we've waited ten years for this, though honestly I never thought it would come. *Real* sequels . . .'

'What's your favorite Star Wars movie?' Gabe asked. Uncharacteristically. Elena looked over at him.

'You might as well ask me who my favorite child is,' Troy said.

'Do you have children?' Elena asked him.

'I meant hypothetically,' Troy said. He exhaled hard. 'This is tough, this is really tough. I'm going to have to go with *The Empire Strikes Back*.'

The next half-hour was taken up by Troy justifying his choice. At several points he considered changing his answer, but he kept landing back on Hoth.

'What about you, Elena?' Gabe finally asked.

She frowned at him. Suspicious. '*Empire*,' she said. 'For all the reasons Troy just said. Plus the kissing. What's yours?'

'*Episode Six*,' Gabe said.

'*Jedi*?' she asked.

He nodded.

'Solid choice,' Troy said. 'Very solid.'

Gabe didn't expound; instead he turned back to Elena. 'So, what's your least favorite?'

'Why do I have to go first?'

'You don't have to,' he said.

She held her coffee cup in both hands. 'No, it's fine. *Jedi*. I still love it. But yeah.'

Troy acted like he'd been shot. '*Jedi*?'

Gabe was shocked, too. 'You think *Episode Six* is worse than *Episode Two*? Worse than Anakin and Padmé frolicking among the shaaks?'

'The shaaks!' Troy said. 'Geonosis!'

Those sounded like nonsense words to Elena. She didn't want to be found out. She bit her lip. 'I wasn't really considering the prequels. You said least *favorite*, not worst.'

'Ahhhh,' Troy said, 'you did say that.'

'True,' Gabe said.

They moved on to Troy's least favorite (*III*—'the violence just struck me as mindless') and then to Gabe's (*II*—'love on the fields of Naboo').

And then Troy had to take a call from his girlfriend.

'So,' Gabe said to Elena, 'who's your favorite character?'

'What are you doing?' Elena said.

'Talking about Star Wars.'

'Why?'

'I thought this was what you wanted.'

'So now you're trying to give me what I want?'

Gabe sighed. 'Not exactly. Just . . . maybe you were right.'

'When?' she asked.

'When you said that the point of being in this line was to be excited about Star Wars with other people who love Star Wars.'

'Of course I was right,' Elena said. 'That's obviously why people camp out like this. Nobody leaves their house to sit outside a theater for a week just so they can ignore other fans.'

'So I was getting in my own way,' Gabe admitted. 'OK?'

'OK,' Elena said carefully.

'So, who's your favorite character?' he asked again.

'You'll probably think it's basic.'

'I'm not a jerk,' he said.

'People who are jerks don't get to decide whether

they're jerks. It's left up to a jury of their peers.'

'I disagree. I do not identify as a jerk, so I'm not going to act like one.'

'Fine,' Elena said. 'Princess Leia.'

'Great choice,' he said.

She was still suspicious. 'What about you?'

The thing about Gabe being nice to Elena for unknown, suspicious reasons was . . . he was still being nice to her. And interesting. And funny. And good company.

She kept forgetting that it was all an act and possibly a ruse—and just enjoyed herself.

They were *all* enjoying themselves.

'Excuse me,' someone said, interrupting a lively discussion about whom they'd each buy a drink for in the cantina.

The whole line looked up. There were two women standing on the sidewalk with bakery boxes. One of them cleared her throat. 'We heard that people were camping out for Star Wars . . .'

'That's us!' Troy said, only slightly less enthusiastically than he'd said it yesterday.

'Where's everybody else?' she asked. 'Are they around the back? Do you do this in shifts?'

'It's just us,' Elena said.

'We're the Cupcake Gals,' the other woman said. 'We thought we'd bring Star Wars cupcakes? For the line?'

'Great!' Troy said.

The Cupcake Gals held on tight to their boxes.

'It's just . . .' the first woman said, 'we were going to take a photo of the whole line, and post it on Instagram . . .'

'I can help you there!' Elena said. Those cupcakes were not going to just walk away. Not on Elena's watch.

Elena took a selfie of their line, the Cupcake Gals and a theater employee all holding Star Wars cupcakes—it looked like a snapshot from a crowd—and promised to post it across all her channels. The lighting was perfect. Magic hour, no filter necessary. *#CupcakeGals #TheForceACAKEns #SalaciousCrumbs*

The Gals were completely satisfied and left both boxes of cupcakes.

'This is the first time I've been happy that there were only three of us,' Elena said, helping herself to a second cupcake. It was frosted to look like Chewbacca.

'You *saved* these cupcakes,' Gabe said. 'Those women were going to walk away with them.'

'I know,' Elena said. 'I could see it in their eyes. I would've stopped at nothing to change their minds.'

'Thank God they were satisfied by a selfie then,' Gabe said. His cupcake looked like Darth Vader, and his tongue was black.

'I'm really good at selfies,' Elena said. 'Especially for someone with short arms.'

'Great job,' Troy said. 'You'll make someone a great provider someday.'

'That day is today,' Elena said, leaning back against the theater wall. 'You're both welcome.'

'Errrggh,' Troy said, kicking his feet out. 'Cupcake coma.'

'How many did you eat?' Gabe asked.

'Four,' Troy said. 'I took down the Jedi Council. Time for a little midday siesta—the Force *asleepens*.'

It was the warmest day yet. Elena wondered if she could take a nap too. Maybe not. It seemed even weirder to be asleep on the street in the middle of the day than at night.

'You hate the prequels more than anyone I've met,' Gabe said, licking his thumb. 'These cupcakes are really good. You should tweet about them again.'

'I don't hate the prequels,' she said.

'We ranked our top thirty characters, and the only prequel character you listed was Queen Amidala.'

That was the only prequel character Elena *knew* . . .

'I mean you must really *hate* them,' he said.

'All right,' she said, 'I feel like I owe you a debt, after you helped me last night—'

'You do,' Gabe said. 'Not quite a life debt. But I did save you from peeing your pants *twice*.'

'So I'm going to tell you a secret,' she said. 'But you have to promise not to use it against me.'

Gabe reached over Elena's legs to get another cupcake. 'How could you possibly have a dark secret involving the Star Wars sequels? Are you responsible for Jar Jar Binks?'

'Do you promise?' she asked.

'Sure, I promise.'

'I've never seen the prequels.'

'*What?*' Gabe spit crumbs all over both of them. Elena shook them out of her ponytail. 'How could that happen?'

'It didn't happen,' she said. 'I never saw them.'

'Was it against your religion? Are you some sort of Star Wars purist?'

'Sort of,' Elena said. 'My dad was. He wouldn't let me see them.'

'Did he lock you in a tower?'

'No. He just told me they were terrible. He said they'd . . . *corrupt* my love of Star Wars.'

'And you never thought of watching them anyway?'

'Not really. It's my *dad*.'

'How does he feel about the sequels? Are you here undercover?'

'I don't know,' Elena said. 'I haven't heard from him.'

Gabe looked confused.

'He's sort of in Florida.'

'"Sort of in Florida" is our band name,' Gabe said.

'Don't tell Troy,' she said.

'I won't. He'd probably make us watch them all on his phone.'

Elena looked down. 'Now you're probably thinking that I really am a fake geek girl.'

'I try not to think that about anybody,' he said. 'If anything, this makes you an uber Star Wars nerd. A Star Wars hipster. You're like one of those people who only listens to music on vinyl.'

'Do you think I should watch the prequels?' she asked.

'How would I know? I mean, I'd watch them. I couldn't know there was more Star Wars out there that I hadn't tapped. You could have double the Star Wars in your life.'

'Did the prequels corrupt your love of Star Wars?'

Gabe gave her a very Han Solo-like grin. 'It was already corrupt, babe.'

They both laughed. This was not the Gabe she'd been sitting next to for two days.

'I don't know,' he said, more seriously. 'I saw the prequels before the original trilogy.'

'What?' It was Elena's turn to be shocked. 'That's all wrong. That's a perversion.'

'It is not!' Gabe said. 'I think it's how George Lucas intended it. It's the higher order.'

'George Lucas doesn't even know what he

intended,' Elena said. 'He can't even decide who shot first.'

'I saw the prequels in the theater,' Gabe said. 'When I was a kid. I thought they were awesome.'

'And now?' she asked.

'They're my first love,' he said. 'I can't be objective.'

Elena hugged herself. 'I don't think I'll ever see them. I feel like I'd be letting my dad down. Like he's going to show up some day, and ask whether I've seen *Attack of the Clones*, and if I say yes, he'll take off again.'

Gabe looked like he was thinking. 'So . . .' he said, 'you won't mind if I spoil them for you.'

'I guess not,' she said. 'I mean, I already know what happens.'

Gabe sat up straight and held both hands up between them. '*Turmoil has engulfed the Great Republic . . .*'

When Troy woke up from his nap, he didn't even ask what they were doing. He just joined in. His Yoda impression was *uncanny*.

'I knew you hadn't seen the prequels,' Troy confided in Elena. 'There were some pretty obvious

gaps in your understanding of the Galactic Senate.'

Troy's girlfriend, Sandra, brought them all pizza that night, and when she got there she joined the dramatic re-enactment. She said they had to rewind so she could elaborate for Elena on how dashing Obi-Wan was. '*Ewan McGregor*,' she groaned. 'I made Troy grow a beard after the second movie.'

'I also grew a Padawan braid,' Troy said.

Troy and Sandra and Gabe acted out a lightsaber battle that brought tears to Elena's eyes, probably because they were all three singing the John Williams music. (Elena knew the prequel music; she'd listened to all the scores.)

Some movie-goers stopped on their way out of the theater to watch. Elena snapped a photo when Gabe fell to the ground. (*#Epic #KnightFall #OnLine)* Everyone clapped.

When the crowd cleared, Elena noticed her mom parked at the curb. Elena jumped up and ran over.

'Are you coming home?' her mom asked.

'Nope,' Elena said. 'Do you want to get in line?'

'No way. You get this craziness from your dad, not me.'

The night was clear and cold. Sandra had talked Manager Mark into refilling Elena's hot-water bottle at the coffee machine. Elena hugged it under her sleeping bag.

'Hey,' Gabe said, 'I got you something.'

'What?'

He handed her a movie-theater cup, one of the new Star Wars ones. 'Tonight you can pee in a collector's item.'

'Ha ha,' Elena said. 'Did we eat all the cupcakes?'

Gabe handed her the box. There was one left. A very lonely C-3PO. Elena picked up her phone and took a photo of it. Then went to Instagram. *#LastDroidStanding*

Her phone battery was still seventy per cent charged, and she only had twenty-four hours to get through, so Elena decided to indulge herself by thumbing through her Instagram feed, reading the comments on her posts from the last few days.

Her friends had all hearted them and left funny

comments. God, Elena missed her friends. (Not that Troy and Gabe weren't great. She'd definitely miss them.) (Even Gabe.) (Especially Gabe.)

Her first post, from Monday, had the most comments. The photo of the line.

'Is that Gabe?' someone had posted.

'GABERS.'

'It's Geekle!' Elena's friend Jocelyn had posted. *'ICKLE GEEKLE.'*

Geekle? Elena thought.

She quickly texted Jocelyn: *'Who's Geekle?'*

'Geekle!' Jocelyn texted back. *'From Spanish class. He sits at the back. He's kind of geeky.'*

'Is that why you call him Geekle?'

'IDK,' Jocelyn sent. *'ICKLE GEEKLE. Tell him I said hi.'*

Elena looked at Gabe. He did look sort of familiar. Now that she thought about it. Jocelyn had nicknames for everyone, usually mean ones. Ickle Geekle, whatever that meant, was mild. Jocelyn herself wasn't very mean, once you got to know her. She just thought she was funnier than she actually was. And she couldn't stand silence. She'd fill every second with stupid jokes.

Gabe. From Spanish class. Elena pictured him

without his peacoat . . . While she was staring, Gabe took off his glasses and rubbed his eyes.

'You don't wear glasses!' she blurted.

'What?' he said, putting his glasses back on.

'In school,' she said. 'You don't wear glasses.'

Gabe's face fell. 'No. I don't.'

Gabe. Geekle. His Spanish name was *Gabriel*. She'd never talked to him; she'd never really looked at him. (Which sounded worse than it was—Elena didn't go around *looking* at people. She minded her own business!)

This was bad. This was very bad.

'I'm sorry,' she said.

'Why?'

'I didn't recognize you.'

'Why would you?' he said.

'We're in class together!'

'You apparently never noticed. There's no crime there.'

'Did you recognize me?'

Gabe turned to look at her. '*Of course.*' He rolled his eyes. 'We've been in school together for four years.'

'I don't know very many people.'

'Why should you?' he said. 'You've got your clique.'

That was true, but not the way he was saying it. 'We're not a clique,' she said.

'Gang, then.'

'Gabe.'

'Army?'

'Why do you dislike us so much?'

'Because you're jerks,' he said. 'Because you call me Geekle—what does that even mean?'

'I don't know. I don't call you that!'

'Because you don't know I exist!'

'I know *now*,' she said.

Gabe started to say something, then shook his head.

'Jocelyn has a big mouth,' Elena said. 'She's harmless.'

'To you,' Gabe said. 'You guys think you're so far above everyone else.'

'I don't think that.'

'You walk around in a clump, looking all cute and matchy, and throw your clever little insults down on us plebes—'

'We never intentionally match!' Elena said.

'Whatever!'

They both sat back, arms crossed.

'It's not like that,' Elena said. 'We're not a clique. We're just friends.'

Gabe huffed. 'Do you know why I know you and your friends? But you don't know me and my friends?'

'Why?'

'Because we don't get in your way. We don't have nicknames for you, and if we did, we wouldn't shout them every day when you walked into Spanish.'

'That's just Jocelyn,' Elena said.

'That's your whole vibe,' Gabe said.

'I don't even have a vibe!'

'Pfft!'

'So you hate me,' she said. 'You hated me before I even got in line.'

'I didn't hate you,' he said. 'You're just . . . part of them.'

'I'm also part of this,' she said.

'What's this? Star Wars? I don't have to like you because you like Star Wars. I don't have to like every meathead with a stormtrooper tattoo.'

'No,' Elena said. 'I'm part of this, part of the line.'

'What does that count for?'

'I don't know,' she said, 'but it should count for something. Look, I'm sorry Jocelyn calls you names. She's a loudmouth. She's been a loudmouth since fourth grade. We're all just *used* to her. And if you've noticed me at all at school, you've noticed that I don't exactly reach out. I don't talk to anybody in some of my classes. There's nobody in my math class who could pick me out of a line-up.'

'I don't believe that,' he said.

'I'm sorry,' she said, 'that I've never talked to you before. But you've never talked to me either. We're talking *now*.'

Gabe gritted his teeth. 'I *hate* it when she calls me Geekle.'

'She calls me Ele-nerd,' Elena said. 'And Short Stuff. Wednesday Addams. Virgin Daiquiri. Ukelena . . . Ukelele. Lele. My Little Pony. Thumbelina. Rumpelstiltskin . . .'

Gabe laughed a little. 'Why do you let her call you all that?'

'I don't even hear it any more,' Elena said. 'Plus it's different. I'm her friend . . . I can have her stop calling you names, if you want?'

'It doesn't even matter,' Gabe said.

They were quiet for a minute. Elena was trying to figure out whether she was mad. She wasn't.

'Why didn't you tell me?' she asked. 'That we already knew each other.'

'I didn't want you to call me Geekle,' Gabe said. 'I didn't want it to catch on.'

Elena nodded.

'We should sleep,' he said. 'This is our last night.'

'Yeah,' Elena said.

He pulled up his legs and folded his arms. *How did he sleep like that?*

Elena curled up as much as she could. She kept trying to get comfortable. It was so bright under the lights.

'Gabe?' she said after ten minutes or so.

'Yeah?'

'Are you asleep?'

'Sort of.'

'Are you still mad?'

Gabe sighed. 'In a larger sense, yes. At you, in this moment, no.'

'OK. Good.'

Elena hunkered down again. She watched the cars driving by. She would be really, really glad to be home tomorrow night. After the movie. The movie . . .

'Gabe?' she said.

'What?'

'I can't sleep.'

'Why not?'

'Star Wars!'

Thursday 17 December 2015

Something strange happened at 6 a.m.

Darth Vader got in line.

It was one of Troy's friends. He kicked Troy's feet off the cooler and shouted, 'The Force awakens!'

'Yeah, we've heard that one,' Gabe grumbled, sitting up.

Elena was watching everything from a gap between her hat and her sleeping bag.

'I haven't slept in a week,' Gabe said. 'I think you can die of that. I think I'm dead.'

Troy woke up and welcomed his friend, who eventually got in line behind Gabe.

Elena and Gabe walked together to Starbucks. She gave him some of her baby wipes; they were both in dire need of a shower. Gabe looked like he was growing a beard. It was coming in redder than his hair. Elena painted new Yodas on her cheeks.

'You into Star Wars?' the barista asked.

'Nope,' Gabe said.

'Yes,' Elena said.

'I'm going to see it tonight,' the barista said. 'Midnight showing.'

'Cool,' Elena said.

'There are already people in line over there,' he said. 'Have you seen them? Just three miserable dorks sitting on the sidewalk.'

Elena smiled brightly. 'That's us!'

'What?'

'We're the three dorks—well, two of the three.'

The barista was mortified; he gave them their coffee for free. 'May the Force be with you!' Elena said.

When they got back, there were three new people in line.

By noon, there were twenty, at least half of them in costume.

By three, there were speakers on the sidewalk, and someone kept playing the victory parade music from *The Phantom Menace* over and over again. (It was only a minute and a half long.)

Elena consented to a ninety-second dance with Troy. Gabe turned him down.

Fifty people showed up by dinner time, and some of them brought pizza. Elena went up and down the line, posing for photos and posting them to Instagram. (Her hashtags were *inspired*.) Troy, who'd changed into his pilot costume, was a little wary of all the newcomers—'Jar-Jar-come-latelies.'

'We have to keep our guard up,' he said. 'These people aren't part of the line covenant. They might try to surge at the end.'

'We still have our tickets,' Gabe said.

'I will be the first person to walk into that theater,' Troy said. 'You will be second. And Elena will be third. We are the line. These are just day guests.'

'So are we sitting together?' Elena asked.

'Oh,' Troy said. 'Well, we can sit near each other. I've actually got a bunch of friends coming . . .'

'We can sit together,' Gabe said, looking at Elena, but somehow *not* looking at Elena. 'If you want.'

'Sure,' she said. 'Let's see this through.'

The newspaper photographer came back. The line wrapped around the block. Mark came out with a loudspeaker to give everybody directions.

'We've got two hours,' Gabe said to Elena. 'I think we've only got time for a tattoo *or* a nickname. Your pick.'

'Let's not talk about nicknames,' she said.

They'd packed up their stuff and Mark said they could leave it in his office during the movie. 'Thank you for not being drunk or disorderly,' he said. 'And for not littering. I hope you camp outside a different theater next time—I'd be happy to make a few recommendations.'

'No chance,' Troy said. 'This is home.'

Elena bounced up and down, pointing from side to side.

'What's that?' Gabe asked.

'It's my Star Wars dance,' she said, bouncing and pointing.

After a few seconds, he joined her. Then Troy's friends picked it up. The dance traveled down the line. From the street, they must have looked like the Peanuts characters dancing.

There *was* a surge at the end—Troy was right! The line turned into a mob when Mark opened the doors. But Mark shouted at everyone and made sure the three original line members got in first. Gabe and Elena grabbed seats in the very middle of the theater.

'Oh my God,' Elena said. 'This is the most comfortable chair I've ever sat in. I feel like a princess.'

'You look like a ruffian,' Gabe said, but his eyes were closed. 'It's so warm,' he said. 'I love inside.'

'Inside is the best,' Elena said. 'Let's never go outside again.'

The theater filled up, and everyone was loud and excited. Elena got a large popcorn and a small pop, and she went to the bathroom twice in the hour before the show started. 'If I have to pee during the movie, I'm using this cup.'

'It's what you do best,' Gabe said.

'I can't believe I made it!' she said. 'I can't believe we're here. I can't believe there's a new Star Wars movie.'

'I can't believe how much I want a shower,' Gabe said.

Elena started doing her Star Wars dance again. It worked just as well in a chair.

When the lights went down, she squealed.

She'd made it. She'd camped out. And she

hadn't given up. And now it was here. Now it was starting.

The opening crawl began. *Episode VII: The Force Awakens.*

Elena felt all the stress and tension—all the adrenalin—of the last four days drain out of her body. She felt like she was sinking deep, deep into the warm, plush chair.

She'd made it. She was here. It was happening.

Friday 18 December 2015

Elena woke up with her head on Gabe's shoulder. In a puddle of spit. Someone was trying to climb over her. 'Excuse me,' the person said. *Why would anyone be leaving during the opening credits?*

The opening credits. There were no opening credits.

Elena looked at Gabe. His head had fallen to the side, and his mouth was open. She shook his arm. *Violently*. 'Gabe, Gabe, Gabe. Wake up! Gabe!'

He sat up like he'd been hit by lightning. 'What?'

'We fell asleep,' Elena said. 'We fell asleep!'

'What?' He looked at the screen—'Oh my God!'—then back at Elena. 'When did you fall asleep?'

'Immediately,' she said. 'As soon as the lights went off. Oh my Gahhhhd.'

'I saw the crawl,' Gabe said. 'And a ship, I think?'

'We missed the whole thing,' Elena said. Her chin was trembling.

'We missed the whole thing,' Gabe repeated.

'We waited for a week, and then we missed the whole thing.' He rested his elbows on his knees and buried his face in his hands. His shoulders started shaking.

Elena laid her hand on him. On the wet spot she'd left on his sleeve. She took her hand back and wiped it on her jeans.

Gabe sat back in his seat with his hands still in his hair. He was laughing so hard he looked like he was in pain.

Elena stared at him, in shock.

And then she started giggling.

And then she started guffawing.

'Elena! Gabe!' Troy was moving with the crowd towards the door. 'Was it everything?'

'I'm speechless!' Elena shouted.

Gabe just kept laughing. 'We slept on the *street,*' he sputtered out. 'You peed in a *dumpster*!'

Elena laughed so hard, her stomach hurt.

There were moments in the laughing when she felt totally miserable and wanted to cry—*she missed the whole thing!*—but that just made her laugh harder.

'What do we do now?' Gabe said. 'Hit the street? Camp out until the next showing?'

'I'm going *home,*' Elena said. 'I'm going to sleep for twelve hours.'

'Good idea,' he said, sobering up a little. 'Me, too.'

Elena looked at him. At his curly brown hair and red stubble. She wondered what he'd look like when he hadn't been sleeping rough for a few days. (She'd know this if she ever picked up her head at school.) 'We could come back tonight,' she said. 'We might be able to get tickets.'

'I actually already have tickets,' Gabe said, running his fingers through his hair. 'I was going to come back at seven and see it again.'

'Oh,' Elena said. 'Cool.'

'You can have one . . .'

'I don't want to take someone else's ticket.'

'It was for my cousin, and he can wait a day,' Gabe said. 'You've been waiting a week.'

'I've been waiting my whole life,' she said.

Gabe smiled at her.

Elena smiled back.

'Meet you tonight?' he said.

Elena nodded. 'First person here gets in line.'

About the Author

Rainbow Rowell lives in Omaha, Nebraska, with her husband and two sons. She's also the author of *Carry On, Fangirl, Attachments, Eleanor & Park,* and *Landline.*

Visit her website at www.rainbowrowell.com

About the Illustrator

Simini Blocker is an illustrator based in Texas. She's always loved drawing characters from her favorite stories.

Find more of her work at siminiblocker.com

Cath and Wren are identical twins and until recently they did absolutely everything together. Now they're off to university and Wren's decided she doesn't want to be one half of a pair any more – she wants to dance, meet boys, go to parties and let loose. It's not so easy for Cath. She would rather bury herself in the fanfiction she writes where there's romance far more intense than anything she's experienced in real life.

FANGIRL

Now Cath has to decide whether she's ready to open her heart to new people and new experiences, and she's realizing that there's more to learn about love than she ever thought possible . . .

RAINBOW ROWELL

CARRY ON

SIMON SNOW IS THE WORST CHOSEN ONE WHO'S EVER BEEN CHOSEN

That's what his roommate, Baz, says. And Baz might be evil and a vampire and a complete git, but he's probably right.

Half the time Simon can't even make his wand work, and the other half, he sets something on fire. His mentor's avoiding him, his girlfriend broke up with him, and there's a magic-eating monster running around wearing Simon's face. Baz would be having a field day with all this, if he were here—it's their last year at the Watford School of Magicks, and Simon's infuriating nemesis didn't even bother to show up.

Edited by STEPHANIE PERKINS